For my sister Patricia,
who made me sing "Little Tommy Tinker"
in front of her class. I haven't sung in public since!
—C.R.

To Molly and Gunnar—
I can always count on you to support Mama
in her art and to never be in short supply of wit,
especially when I'm at my wit's end.
Dream BIG, my loves! (Thanks, Elaine.)
—C.G.

Text copyright © 2017 by Candice Ransom
Jacket art and interior illustrations copyright © 2017 by Christine Grove

All rights reserved. Published in the United States by Doubleday, an imprint of Random House Children's Books,
a division of Penguin Random House LLC, New York.

Doubleday and the colophon are registered trademarks of Penguin Random House LLC.

Visit us on the Web! randomhousekids.com

Educators and librarians, for a variety of teaching tools, visit us at RHTeachersLibrarians.com

Library of Congress Cataloging-in-Publication Data
Names: Ransom, Candice F., author. | Grove, Christine, illustrator.
Title: Amanda Panda quits kindergarten / by Candice Ransom ; illustrated by
Christine Grove.
Description: First Edition. | New York : Doubleday, [2017] |
Summary: When Amanda Panda's first day of kindergarten does not go according to plan,
she decides to quit and join her older brother in the second grade.
Identifiers: LCCN 2016001228 | ISBN 978-0-399-55455-1 (hc) |
ISBN 978-0-399-55456-8 (glb) | ISBN 978-0-399-55457-5 (ebk)
Subjects: | CYAC: Kindergarten—Fiction. | First day of school—Fiction. |
Schools—Fiction. | Pandas—Fiction.
Classification: LCC PZ7.R1743 Am 2017 | DDC [E]—dc23

MANUFACTURED IN CHINA
10 9 8 7 6 5 4 3 2 1
First Edition

Amanda Panda
QUITS KINDERGARTEN

by Candice Ransom
illustrated by Christine Grove

DOUBLEDAY BOOKS FOR YOUNG READERS

Amanda Panda's favorite color is brown.

She wants to be a school bus driver when she grows up.

She can run really fast, but only downhill.

And she cannot wait to start kindergarten.

When she gets to school, she will print her name in big, important letters on the board so the whole class will know who she is.

Next, she will build the tallest block tower.

Finally, she will run the fastest of anyone.

Her brother, Lewis, did all those things when he was in kindergarten.

Amanda will do them, too.

On the first day of school,
she buttons her best dress.

She slips Hartley, her favorite
rock, into her backpack.

She ties her zippiest sneakers.

"No hair bows," she tells her
mother.

Ribbons will just slow
Amanda down.

Lewis leaves for school
without her.
"Wait!" cries Amanda.
She races to catch up, but
it's uphill.
"I'm meeting my friends,"
he says.

At the bus stop is a
girl in head-to-toe pink.
So much pink it gives
Amanda a headache.

Amanda claims the seat behind the bus driver so she can watch him steer.

Something very pink sits beside her.

"I'm Bitsy," says Bitsy. "I like all the colors on your dress."

It would be kind to return the compliment.

"My favorite color is sparkles!" Bitsy adds.

Amanda Panda does not feel like being kind. She looks out the window and studies the roads.

At school, Amanda dashes to
Room One. Bitsy is already there.
"Daisies!" says Ms. Lemon,
their teacher. "Bitsy, how sweet!"

Amanda finds a desk close to the board.
Near the Building Center, far from Bitsy.
Something very pink slides next to her.
"Neighbors!" says Bitsy.
It is the end of the world.

Molly Thomas Gunnar Jill Bitsy Sofi James Anna Lou Sally Andrew Nan Lilly

"Let's print our names on the board," Ms. Lemon says.
"We'll get to know each other."

Amanda waves her hand, but Bitsy goes first.

She prints BITSY in big, important letters in the middle
of the board.

When Amanda is called, there is only one little corner left.
No one can see her name.

Next, it's Building Center time.
Amanda grabs the large blocks. She stacks
block upon block in a tall, teetering tower.
"I'm making a Kitty Castle," says Bitsy.
"How sweet!" says Ms. Lemon.

Ms. Lemon frowns. "Not so many blocks, Amanda."

At recess, Amanda sprints past Bitsy,
who plays princess with the other girls.
"Race you," she challenges Jasper.
"To the swings," he says. "Get set, GO!"
Amanda is wearing her zippiest sneakers.
And the swings are downhill. She'll win, easy.

But then Amanda trips over a princess. Her knees hit the ground.

Bitsy hurries over. "Are you okay?"

Amanda is not okay. She lost the race. Her tower fell. And no one knows who she is, except Bitsy.

"Why are you wearing flowers?" Amanda asks.

"I'm Head Princess," says Bitsy.

It is definitely the end of the world.

Ms. Lemon's whistle shrills.
Recess is over.

Amanda does not want to go back to class.

She does not want to be in kindergarten anymore.

"Line up," Ms. Lemon says. "A line, please, not a mob."

Suddenly, Amanda has a plan.

No one sees Amanda switch lines. No one sees her go down the main hall and turn left. No one sees her walk into Lewis's classroom.

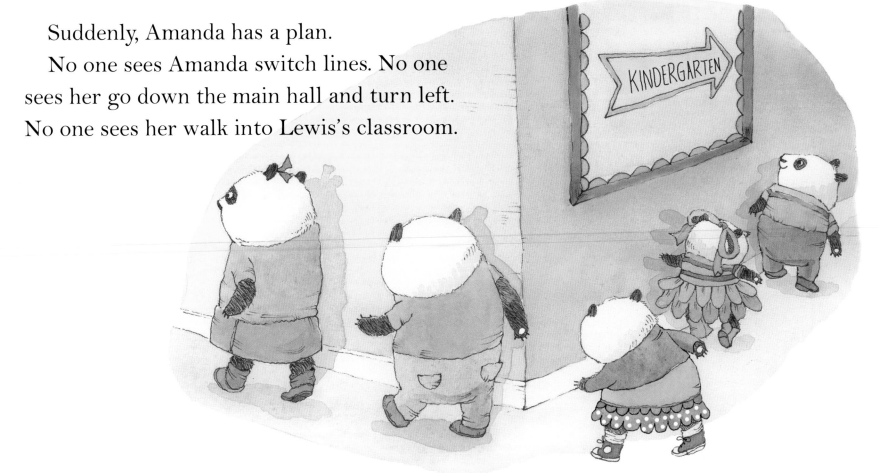

Amanda takes an empty seat beside her brother.
"What are *you* doing here?" he whispers.
"I quit kindergarten," says Amanda.

The second-grade room is very quiet. Everyone is reading.

The chairs are big and her feet don't touch the floor. There are hard words on the board that she can't read. There is no Building Center.

Amanda's stomach feels cold.

"Can I help you, dear?"

Lewis's teacher asks her.

always
around
been
before
does
fast

"Yes!" Something very pink sobs in the doorway.

"Oh, my," Lewis's teacher says. "Are all the kindergartners in the wrong room today?"

"Bitsy, what are *you* doing here?" asks Amanda.

"I tried to find you but then I got lost and now I'll never see Ms. Lemon and my Kitty Castle again!"

Bitsy looks so small and helpless.

"You quit kindergarten to find me?" says Amanda.

Bitsy hiccups.

"Don't worry. I've got this," Amanda says to Lewis's teacher.

She hops out of the chair and skips to the door.

Amanda takes Bitsy's hand, turns right,
then leads her down the main hall.
It does not hurt one bit to be kind.
And second grade can wait.

No one notices they are late.

Amanda slides into her seat. Her sneakers tap comfortably on the floor. On the board, her name seems to sparkle.

Bitsy sits next to her.

"Thanks," Bitsy says. "I want you to have this."

Bitsy's pink hair bow is a burst of bright color against Amanda's white fur.

Suddenly, Amanda thinks of a new plan.

Tomorrow she will build a garage for Bitsy's kittens. And she will try to run halfway up the hill.

"Neighbors?" Bitsy says.

"Friends," says Amanda.

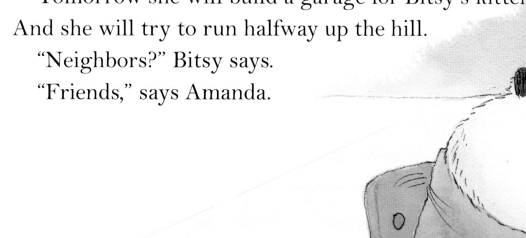

And it is not the end of the world.

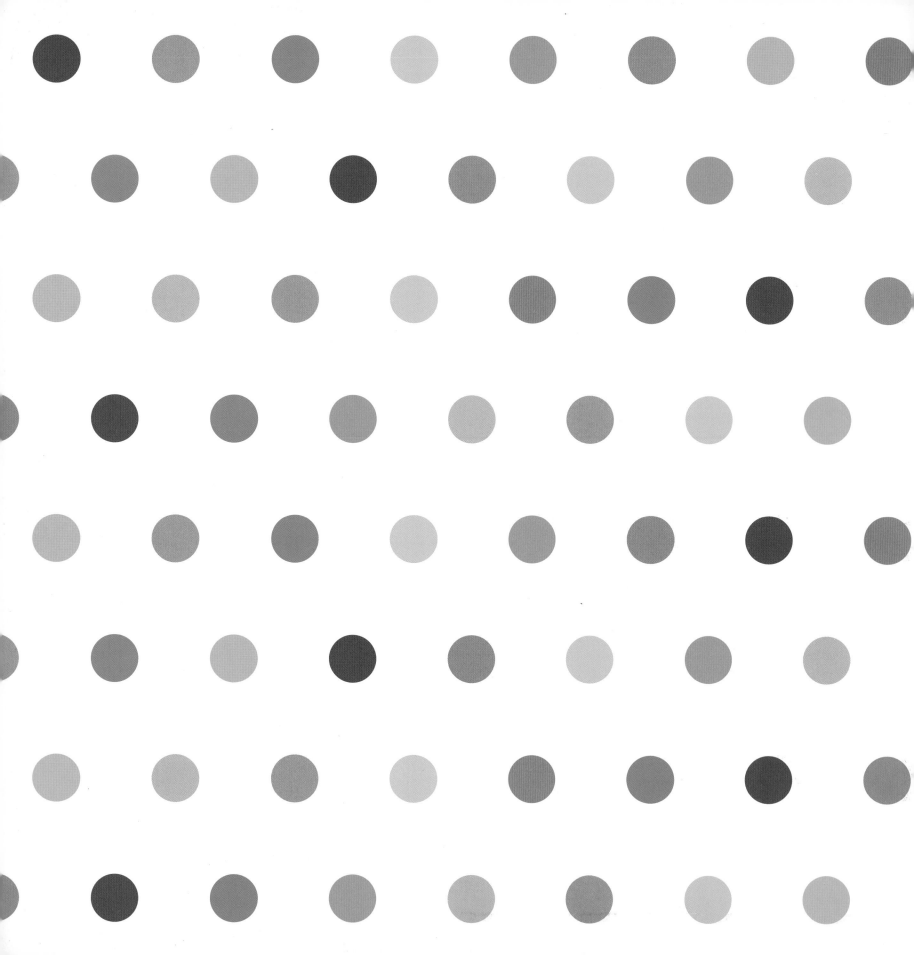